DOUBLE BREASTED

CAPRICORN COVE

EVIE MITCHELL

THUNDER THIGHS PUBLISHING

Editor: Nicole Wilson, Evermore Editing

ACKNOWLEDGEMENT OF COUNTRY

I acknowledge the Traditional Custodians of the lands on which I write, the Ngunnawal people, and pay my respect to elders both past and present.

I acknowledge the continued and deep spiritual relationship of the Australian Aboriginal and Torres Strait Islander peoples' to this land, and their unique cultural and spiritual relationships to the land, waters and seas and their rich contribution to society.

Always was, always will be.

*As always to my husband,
the real MVP for putting up with chicken jokes
while I wrote this book.*

*And for Min.
I'll be your wing bitch any time.
Wing, get it? I crack myself up.*

DOUBLE BREASTED

Willodean

I moved back to Capricorn Cove to escape the daily grind of the city and be closer to my brother and sister and their growing families.

So, what did I do? I bought a chicken farm,

Yep. I traded in suits and briefcases for overalls and gumboots. It sounded like a good idea at the time.

And it was. For all of five minutes. That's how long it for me to figure out that my chickens are Satan's minions as they tried to burn down the barn.

Worst day ever. Or at least, it was.

Enter Teresa 'Teddy' Prince. The hottest firefighter I've ever clapped eyes on and my newest crush.

Perhaps my chickens weren't so bad after all...

Teresa

When meeting the woman I might want to spend the rest of my life with I expected sparks, not a goddamned fire.

Willow is funny, creative, intriguing – and available.

But I've been burned before, and I know she's hiding something. After all, no one just up and buys a chicken farm... right?

Warning: This book is inspired by strong women, crazy chickens, and hot summer nights. So, get thee a partner, some lingerie, and settle in — this book is bound to ruffle your feathers.

PROLOGUE

Willodean

I stared at the invitation in my hands.

Oh, Baby!

You're invited to a (virtual) baby shower honouring Honey Rodriguez on August 14.

"Oh damn."

August 14th, my surgery date.

I swallowed, running a hand through my hair and grimacing when strands clung to my sweaty skin, before falling to the floor.

You have to tell them. You can't hide it anymore.

I looked up, catching a glimpse of myself in my hallway mirror. Outside, cars drove past, the noise of the city only slightly muted by the heavy door and insulated walls of my brownstone.

My blonde hair looked limp, greasy, and patchy. Dark circles and pale skin completed the unhealthy picture.

Chemotherapy was kicking my ass.

Six months ago, on the eve of my sister's wedding, I'd noticed some weird rash on my breast. Assuming it was just an allergy, I'd put off seeing a doctor for a few weeks.

The rash had turned out to be inflammatory breast cancer. An aggressive form of cancer that we had to treat aggressively in turn. Chemotherapy, mastectomy, more chemo, and even some hormone therapy. I was lucky. I'd managed to catch it early enough to avoid hitting stage four but was still at stage 3B – or what I called the shit-hitting-the-fan stage.

The cancer had spread to my mammary lymph nodes but no, thankfully, to other parts of my body. It was late enough that it had caused damage but early enough that I had an excellent chance at recovery.

I remembered getting home after the specialist appointment, unwrapping my scarf from around my neck, and dropping onto the couch beside my girlfriend, Lou.

"You okay?" she'd asked, as she flicked through the channels on our TV.

"Umm..."

She'd settled on an old Judge Judy replay, laughing when Judy rolled her eyes at the witness.

"I love Judy. She's the best."

I cleared my throat, trying to pull myself together.

"Lou... there's something I need to tell you."

She'd turned to me, her expression interested but not alarmed.

"I have breast cancer."

We'd cried together on the couch still sat in my living room. We'd sobbed and made pledges. We'd agreed to do whatever was necessary to get me through this. Then we'd gone to bed, making frantic love – the kind people did when they realised life was precious and had learned just how breakable they were.

I'd woken, gone to work, and returned home to find Lou gone. All her possessions and presence scrubbed from our house. She'd even taken our cat.

On the counter had been a note with just two words.

I'm sorry.

The blow had been devastating, but I'd worked through it even as I'd hesitated to reveal my life-changing news to anyone.

When the pandemic hit, I'd had an excuse to hide in my brownstone. I'd worked from home when I could, but more often than not found myself puking into a toilet bowl after a chemo session. I'd hired a live-in nurse, appreciating Maddison's no-nonsense attitude.

I was just about to wind up my first six-month chemo session. I had a tentative surgery date of the fourteenth of August for my mastectomy.

I swallowed, bile burning the back of my throat.

My hair had held out the longest. Perhaps because it was so thick. Or maybe I'd just been lucky. But looking in the mirror, I couldn't blame the dark circles and pale skin on late nights in the office anymore. I had to tell the truth.

My sister is having a baby, and I'm about to lose my breasts.

I blew out a breath.

"Alexa, what time is it in Capricorn Cove?"

The little machine blinked, registering my question. "It's 7:04 p.m. in Capricorn Cove."

I swallowed again, turning away from my hall mirror to find Maddison staring at me, her expression knowing.

"Is it finally time?" she asked.

I blinked back tears, my throat working rapidly.

She came down, putting an arm around my shoulders in a motherly gesture. "I'll be right here with you."

She settled me on the hateful couch where I'd first vocalised my diagnosis, then handed me my cell.

"Go on, call your family."

With a deep breath, I pressed dial.

"Hey, sis! You must be psychic cause Cal and Emily just turned up!" Honey laughed down the phone.

I closed my eyes, both cursing my timing and unreasonably grateful that I could tell most of my family this news in one hit.

"Honey, can you put me on speaker?" I asked, my voice sounding weak.

"Sure, hang on a second." There was a fumbling then my brother's warm voice came over the line.

"How are you doing up there in New York, Willow?" he asked, sounding worried and exasperated with me. "Those infection numbers are starting to look a little better."

While the majority of the world measured their lives by infection rates of COVID-19 or days in lockdown, I measured mine by the spaces between chemotherapy sessions and blood tests. By the number of hairs I found on my pillow, and needles that pressed into my delicate skin.

"Guys, I...." My voice broke, fleeing me.

Maddison squeezed my hand, her old eyes warm and understanding.

"Willow?" Tristan, my sister's husband, called my name. "You okay, sis?"

I broke, tears flooding down my cheeks. The weight of months of lies lifted as I finally admitted my darkest secret.

"I have breast cancer."

I began to sob and handed the phone to Maddison, who took over, introducing herself and rapidly filling my family in on my condition, my treatment, and what came next.

"I... I'm sorry," I sobbed down the phone. "I can't m-m-make it to your b-b-baby shower."

Honey made a distressed sound. "As if I care about baby showers when you're ill."

It took hours, but finally, my family agreed to stay put. I didn't want them putting themselves at risk of infection just to fly across the ocean to be with me.

I finally hung up, wrung out and exhausted.

Maddison brushed stray hairs from my flushed skin. "Do you feel better?" she asked me, her weathered face wrinkled with concern.

I sighed, closing my eyes. "No. But now they know."

She reached out, clutching my hand between both of hers. "And you have another thing to look forward to."

I raised an eyebrow.

"A baby. A niece."

"Niece?" I asked, my lips twitching despite my exhaustion. "Pretty sure Honey explicitly said they didn't want to know the sex."

Maddison flapped her hands at me. "I saw your sister's latest pregnancy pictures. My three daughters all carried exactly the same way with their girls. Mark my words. It's a niece."

I looked down at my breasts, feeling a weird mix of maddening grief. "I'll never breastfeed."

Maddison said nothing, just let me speak.

My heart felt heavy. I wanted my sister. My brother. I wanted to be surrounded by family who loved me and wanted to shower me with support. I wanted to be Auntie Willow. I wanted to cuddle my niece or nephew and smell their little head.

I wanted to go home.

"I... I think I want to move back to the Cove."

Maddison nodded, squeezing my hand. "Once this is over, and the doctor gives you the okay, I'll help you pack."

My chin wobbled, and my eyes, the traitorous bitches, filled with fresh tears. "And I need to shave my hair."

Maddison just nodded matter-of-factly, accepting that I knew it was time.

"And... Maddison?"

She cocked an eyebrow at me.

"I'm gonna kick this cancer's butt."

She grinned, slapping me on the shoulder. "Damn straight."

1

Willodean

Two years later

"And remember, you can call anytime if you have any issues," Mrs. Regis reminded me. "We're only down the road."

I nodded, holding the door to her ancient car as she climbed in. "Don't worry about me, you've been a fabulous help. I'm sure I'll be fine."

She paused staring at me for a moment then shook her head, muttering, "City girls." With that ringing endorsement, she turned to her husband. "Drive, Phil."

I shut the door, waving as the couple took off, finally leaving me in peace.

It's not that I didn't appreciate their assistance, I really did. But when I'd purchased the chicken farm I hadn't expected them to stay another month after settlement.

"We'll stay and train you, dear," Mrs. Regis, the smiling assassin, had told me with a little pat to my arm. "Chicken farming ain't as easy as we make it look."

Regis eggs were a local institution. The farm produced eggs that were transported to every seller in town and select restaurants around the state.

"Happy chickens," Mrs. Regis had explained over a delicious quiche one night. "Produce the best eggs. It's the joy you can taste."

While I was sure that had to be true, it didn't hurt that they had cultivated a flock of poultry that won awards year-round.

But the Regis' were getting on in years, and their kids had no interest in carrying on the farm, so they'd listed it for sale.

I'd been in my final month of my final round of chemotherapy, sitting in a cold hospital room with a bald head and still healing chest, when I'd stumbled across their listing.

Perhaps it was the fact I'd just had both

breasts removed. Perhaps it was the weather. Or perhaps it was the offhanded comment my mother had made about my appearance earlier that week—asking if I would consider wearing a wig to make my health issues less obvious. Whatever the reason, I'd done the unthinkable. I'd called the real estate agent and put in an offer. I'd quit my job that afternoon, put my townhouse on the market, booked a one way ticket back to Astir, rented a tiny beach bungalow down the street from my sister, and moved back to Capricorn Cove while I recovered.

Maddison had come for the first few months, but after getting the all-clear from my surgeon and celebrating with tears and champagne, she'd patted me on the shoulder, packed up her things, and left to return to the States and help her next patient.

She still texted me every night to remind me to eat vegetables with dinner. Gods bless her heart.

Back in the Cove, I'd waited with anxious breath while the homeowners had taken their time deciding whether to accept my offer. After some toing-and-froing, they'd finally accepted. And last month, I'd finally taken ownership of the farm.

Today would be my first day alone – Mr. and

Mrs. Regis having finally determined that I was a capable enough farmer for them to move into their son's garage apartment full-time.

Gods help them.

Though I had no doubt Mrs. Regis would be back to cluck over her brood at some point in the near future.

As their car disappeared down the long driveway, I turned back to survey my new home. The old ranch needed repairs and updates, but the sheds were in perfect condition. There was a large barn, including a cold room, which was where the eggs were stored and packaged before pick-up. Off the barn was a small office and break room for the workers. The chickens were all free-range, which meant there were three gigantic moveable coops which circled the large property, encouraging the birds to diversify their diet. The entire property was surrounded by a predator-proof fence that required daily checks.

Tomorrow my employees would arrive, and we'd get to work collecting eggs and sorting production. But today, I wanted to enjoy the quiet sunny Sunday.

I headed inside, pouring myself a cup of coffee and snagging a book from my shelf before taking a seat on the porch swing.

Sucking in a deep breath I closed my eyes, breathing in my surroundings.

Peace.

For the first time in forever I felt at peace. Sure, life at the farm would no doubt be crazy. But today, in this moment, I had exactly what I was searching for.

Or at least I did until I took my first sip of coffee.

An alarm split the air, wailing across the yard.

Startled, I splashed coffee on myself as I stood, gasping as I caught sight of the black smoke billowing from one of the sheds.

Wait. What!?

"Fuck!" I sprang to my feet, my mug tumbling with a crash to the porch as I leapt to the ground. "Oh God, please, no!"

The shed was off to the side of my main yard and stored things to run the packing machinery. Things like oil, gas, and other chemicals.

"Oh shit." I skidded to a halt, staring at the flames licking the roof of the shed. A small flock of escapee chickens, led by a large black rooster, fluttered about in a panic.

"Houdini!" I howled at the rooster, heading to the shed. "What the fuck did you do?!"

The smoke alarm was routed to automatically alert the local fire department. I just needed to contain the spread as much as possible until they arrived.

I pulled the fire extinguisher from the wall, quickly reading the tag, coughing as the smoke filled my lungs.

"Pull the pin, aim, squeeze slowly, sweep from side to side," I read, following the instructions. "And try not to fucking panic!"

I squeezed the lever, sweeping to cover the flames in foam. It seemed to work for about two minutes then the fire came back, roaring as it caught a can of gasoline.

"Nope, I'm out."

I tossed the extinguisher to the side, backing up to what I felt was a safe distance as the flames began to consume the shed.

"Five minutes, Willow. Five fucking minutes you've been alone on this farm and you already burn a shed down." I crossed my arms over my chest, shock setting in. "Jesus, this was a terrible idea."

The familiar wail of the fire engine drew closer and I turned, watching them roar down my drive, coming to a stop a little way from me.

"Anyone inside?" a man asked as he leaped from the truck.

"No, it's just me today."

He nodded. "Anything we should know about in there?"

"It's a storage shed, gasoline, likely other flammable and explosive chemicals."

"Gotcha."

They worked quickly, the team laying foam down to settle the fire. One of them backed me up, explaining that they were using oxygen as they weren't yet sure if the smoke was hazardous.

Great, another item to add to my list of things-that-might-kill-Willow.

It took about an hour for them to extinguish the flames and comb through the rubble, making sure no embers hid in the stinking, smoking wreck.

I could practically see the money disappearing from my account when the insurance agency heard about this.

Farewell, low premiums.

I'd pulled myself together enough to go looking for Houdini and his flock. I found them pecking at a patch of clover behind the herb garden. I'd bribed them with handfuls of corn, and managed to get them back down to their hutch. I'd expected some disaster, like a foxhole or ripped-off side that had enabled their escape. Instead, the door to the hutch was unhinged, swaying uselessly in the breeze.

"Oh, for Gods sake." I threw a handful of corn in the hutch, shifting as the chickens darted toward the delicious treat. Once safely inside, I shut the door, double-checking the latch.

Mr. Regis had been responsible for feeding this lot this morning, but I didn't want to assign blame. Shit happened, and you just dealt with it.

Don't I know it?

With the chickens taken care of, though I had no doubt the stressed hens wouldn't be laying for a few days, I headed back up to the house and the waiting questions from the firefighters.

The guy who'd secured the scene earlier fell into step beside me.

"We're just checking for the source of the fire." He nodded at the charred corpse of the shed. "We should be done in about an hour."

I blew out a breath, running my hand down my face, grimacing when it came away smudged with ash.

"Thanks." I nodded at the assembled crew. "Can I get you guys some coffee, or water, or... something?"

"Water would be great, thanks. And sorry to be the bearer of bad news, but the police will be here shortly. They'll want a statement."

I huffed out a laugh. "Great. The in-laws are descending."

"In-law—?" He was cut off by the screaming wail of police sirens.

With all lights blazing and siren on full, the patrol car careened down my drive, skidding to a halt beside the fire truck. My brother-in-law, Sheriff Tristan Rodriguez, leapt from the car.

"Willodean! What happened? Are you okay? Do you need an ambulance?"

I shook my head. "I'm fine, Tristan. The only damage is the shed and a few ruffled feathers."

He pulled me in for a hug, giving me a tight squeeze. "Thank God. Wasn't sure how I'd be able to tell Honey about this one."

"Something, something, Willow was killed by her chickens?" I asked.

He let me go with a final squeeze. "I told you chickens were to be feared."

Tristan, I'd learned, had an aversion to my feathered friends. Something to do with a childhood run-in with a rooster. At the last dinner party hosted by Honey and Tristan, I'd tried to get the story from Wolf, Tristan's younger brother, but he'd been unable to communicate, he'd laughed so hard.

I will find out one day.

He gave me a once-over. "Weren't the Regis' leaving today?"

I laughed, nodding. "It's taken me a whole year to get to this point, and on my first day alone, there's a fire. How is this my life?"

A throat cleared behind me.

"Sheriff, a word?"

We turned, and my heart went boom.

Oh. Wow.

2

Teddy

hy does she have to be attractive?

The homeowner looked a little worse for wear but no less stunning. Ash peppered her short spunky, blonde pixie cut, her casual jeans, and simple black crew neck shirt. Her skin was slightly flushed, her big blue eyes framed by long as-hell lashes. I'd have assumed she was a catwalk model if not for her boots which were thick, scuffed, and a little muddy.

Don't lose sight of the issue.

"Teresa," Tristan greeted me, placing a hand on the woman's back, guiding her closer. "This is my sister-in-law, Willodean Jameson. Willow, this is Teresa Prince. She's the captain of this crew and our local fire investigator. You'll need her report for your insurance."

The woman, Willow, held out a hand, her smile easy. "Nice to meet you, Teresa. Sorry, it had to be under such dramatic circumstances."

I gripped her hand, noticing how smooth her palm was. Heat swept up my arm from where our skin touched.

"I go by Teddy," I corrected, knowing I sounded like an idiot.

Willow nodded as if tucking away that information.

We dropped hands, and I tucked mine in my pockets, clearing my throat. "Sheriff, if I could steal you for a minute?"

Tristan followed me back to the burned-out shed, letting out a low whistle when he saw what was left of the structure.

"Accelerant came from a can of poorly stored gasoline." I pointed to a melted area in the remains of the shed. "We're still looking at ignition points." I hesitated, knowing I had to ask but frustrated by the nerves that fluttered in my stomach.

"Sheriff, I have to ask. Is Ms. Jameson experiencing any financial difficulties?"

Tristan blinked, absorbing my words. "Wait... financial... you think she did this?"

I tucked my hands into my pockets, trying to remain casual. "Just covering all bases."

Tristan threw back his head, laughter pouring out of him so hard his body shook with it.

Well. That's not the reaction I was expecting.

He calmed, grin firmly in place. "Sorry, it's just... Teddy, Willow's a fucking millionaire. She was a financial advisor. The woman has more money than half this town combined."

"Jesus." I looked around. "Why'd she buy a pokey chicken farm?"

Tristan hesitated, and I got the sense he was choosing his words carefully before answering.

"Health issues. She wanted to reduce her stress."

I looked pointedly at the smoldering remains of the shed.

His lips twitched. "Believe it or not, she's actually the one with the lowest drama in this family."

I laughed, shifting in place.

Between Tristan's rockstar brother, Wolf, who was currently touring Europe with his band, and his brother-in-law's wife, who'd suffered amnesia, the Rodriguez-Jameson crew had some kooky drama going on.

"Okay, so it's unlikely to be insurance fraud."

Tristan chuckled. "If Willow's trying to commit insurance fraud, then I'll eat my pistol."

I rolled my eyes. "Is Ms. Jameson gonna be okay for me to interview?"

He nodded. "Yeah, she'll be good. She's good in a crisis."

We headed back to the house, finding my guys sharing mugs of coffee and shooting the breeze with Willow.

Seeing her laugh, I was struck once again by her beauty. I didn't normally go for women with short hair, I preferred to wrap their locks around my hands when I kissed them. But Willow worked that pixie cut and her face was... incredible. Striking. Stunning.

Too bad she was currently my lead suspect.

Gods damn it.

I cleared my throat, absently brushing my dark braid over my shoulder as I headed her way.

"Ms. Jameson," I interrupted the mirth of the moment. "Is there somewhere private we can go for an interview?"

Willow locked her big blue eyes on me, her gaze warm and completely unconcerned.

In my line of work – even in a small town like Capricorn Cove – you met enough shitty people to be able to place them.

Willow was not a shitty person. Not by any stretch of the imagination.

Pull it together, Teddy!

"Of course, this way." Willow turned on her heel, leading me into her house.

"Uh...." I hesitated in the doorway, blinking at the giant rooster painted on her wall. "That's... unusual."

"It's a giant cock, and I can assure you it will be one of the first things I remove when I gut this kitchen." Willow laughed, gesturing at me to take a seat at her kitchen table.

As I moved to sit, I couldn't help but notice the place had chicken curtains, chicken tiles, and the odd (and quite terrifying) painted chicken's head poking out from behind shelves or cabinets.

"Don't worry, you can laugh," Willow told me, pouring us each a glass of lemonade from a pitcher on her table. "I would, only I have to live with the damned things until the contractors come to rip it all out in a few months."

I hid a grin, pulling a notepad and pen from my pocket and placing my cell on the table between us. "You mind if I record this?"

She set the glass before me, shaking her head. "Go ahead."

I hit the recording app, checking it was good.

"Okay. Here we go. Interview with Ms. Willodean Jameson at the Regis Poultry Farm at..." I checked my watch. "Thirteen-forty-three."

I held up my pen, looking at Willow. "Ms. Jameson, can you take me through the events from today's fire?"

"It's Willow, and sure." She walked me through her morning with the Regis' before describing seeing the smoke and running to get the extinguisher.

"And the chickens were where exactly?" I asked, my mind racing as I pieced together the scene.

"All over. Houdini, he's the rooster that giant mosaic is based on. Anyways, Houdini was inside with some of his hens, the rest were running around terrified outside. It wasn't until I went in and saw the fire that he led his women out, and they all took off."

I nodded, making a note to check for chicken carcasses.

"And after that?"

"I got the extinguisher and tried to put it out." Her lips curved into a self-deprecating smile. "That was a big ass failure. So I backed up and waited for you guys."

"But you didn't call it in?"

She shook her head. "Didn't have to. The newly installed system does it all for me. I figured I'd be better off making sure it didn't spread than trying to head back to the house to call."

"I noticed cameras on each of the main buildings. Do you have one for this shed?"

Her eyes lit, widening as she laughed. "Shit, yeah. Oh God, I'm so sorry. I should have offered this before." She pulled out her mobile, her fingers flying across the screen.

"It's all stored in the cloud these days. That way investigators can make sure nothing's been tampered with." She handed over the phone, pointing at a flashing icon. "Hit that, it'll play the video at double speed and start from about thirty minutes before I noticed the fire."

Our hands brushed, sparks jumping between us.

With a slight flush, I dipped my head, tapped the button then watched the screen. Nothing appeared on the screen for the first few minutes then a small flock of chickens strolled through the open side of the shed, pecking at the ground. The rooster ran in, chasing one of the hens. Another few minutes passed with no major incident until the rooster ran at the hen again, causing it to take flight and flap as it jumped onto a gas can, knocking the lip slightly off.

Well, that answers one question.

Attached to the wall beside the canister was a wire. Another chicken began pecking at the wire, and after a moment, I had my answer as to how the fire began – fried chicken.

The electrocuted chicken had conducted enough energy between it and the gas can to generate a small spark. The gas had caught, setting fire to a pallet leaning on the wall beside the can. Within five minutes, the shed was ablaze, and Willow was desperately trying to put it out.

I hit pause when the video cut out, no doubt the power to the cameras had been destroyed in the blaze.

"Can you send this to me?" I asked, handing her back her phone.

"Of course. I'll have to download it, though, if that's okay?"

I nodded, making notes in my pad. "Of course."

Willow remained quiet while I filled out my paper, checking the time and dates and double-checking the spelling of her name.

Satisfied with my report, I signed at the bottom of the form, finally looking up. She watched me, a small smile on her lips.

Down, Teddy!

This woman made me feel like a schoolgirl,

my traitorous nipples pebbling every time I looked at her.

"If you stop by the station tomorrow, I'll have my report typed up for you. Your insurance company may want a copy of this and the video, but it seems pretty open and close."

She nodded, palming her glass between her two hands. "Thank you, and your men, for coming out. I really appreciate it."

I pushed to stand, handing her my card. "It's no problem. It's actually our job."

Her lips curved up into a generous smile. "Still, thank you."

I gave her a brisk nod, collecting my things. "Right... well. Tomorrow."

~

BACK AT THE STATION, I typed up the report and handed a printed copy to my deputy to check.

"Looks good," Ren said, signing at the bottom. "You want me to scan this and send it off?"

I coughed, feeling my face flush. "Umm, actually, she's coming in to pick it up."

Ren froze, his eyebrows lifting. "Excuse me? Is this 1985, and we work in paper now, Captain?"

I tried not to fidget but failed miserably. "It's

not that big a deal, Ren. I just forgot to ask for her email."

"And the fact that she's...." He lifted a hand, ticking off a list on his fingers. "One, new to town. Two, obviously the hottest woman we've seen in years. Thr—"

"Oh, fuck off." I threw a pen at him, which he easily caught, tucking it behind his ear with a snigger. "Besides, she's probably got a partner."

He chuckled, "Captain. The woman had a fire, and the only person who showed up was her brother-in-law. Your woman calls to say she's had a fire, what would you do?"

"I'd be headed home ASAP."

He slapped a hand on the table. "Exactly."

I nodded, considering his words. "So, you're saying go for it?"

He grinned. "If you don't, I will."

I rolled my eyes. "Look, you may be a cocky bastard, but I'm hot as fuck. And I speak woman. There'd be no competition."

He laughed. "That's true."

I pulled the signed report from his desk, folding it, and headed back to my office. "See you tomorrow, Ren."

"Night, Captain. Sweet dreams."

I shook my head as I heard him laugh at his own joke.

"Idiot."

3

Willow

I hesitated, wondering for the fiftieth time if this was a terrible idea.

"Come on, Willow. It's just thank-you brownies," I muttered to myself, shifting the Tupperware container from one hand to the other. "Not a marriage proposal."

Rationally, I knew this. But it'd been a long time since I'd had even a flutter of attraction toward another person.

And Teresa Prince, with her dark brunette hair, piercing eyes, and begrudging smile, had managed to ruffle my feathers.

You really need to stop with the chicken puns.

I sucked in a breath, straightened my shoulders, and strode headfirst into the fire station.

Behind the redwood entry door lay a white and black tiled foyer, battered wooden reception desk, and solid brick and tile walls.

It may surprise people to learn that even though my brother-in-law was the town's Sheriff, I didn't make a habit of visiting emergency departments. In fact, apart from the police station open day last month (that I only attended because Honey needed me to look after my niece while she manned the bake sale), I couldn't think of one other instance where I'd been in a station – police, ambulance or fire.

"Hello?" I called, peeking around the seemingly empty room. "Is anyone in here?"

A head poked out from a hallway, the guy doing a double take when he saw me standing there.

"Wow! I totally thought you were a ghost." His head disappeared before he came back out, his big body clad in a blue shirt, dark trousers, and heavy boots. "Hey, I'm Ren."

I juggled the brownies, giving him a nod. "Nice to meet you."

He eyed the container. "Is that for me?"

I laughed, handing it over. "Actually, it was for Captain Prince." I felt a flush creep up my neck. "I mean... if she's around. And not allergic to gluten or dairy. Or a vegan. Or—"

Ren cut me off. "Nah, you're good. I think

the only thing she's allergic to is winning at poker."

"Oh, shove off." Teddy entered the room, her braid bounced in time with her walk. I took a moment to admire the picture she presented – skin still slightly tan, no doubt from a summer spent outside, hair shiny and soft-looking, her grin welcoming and genuine.

She's stunning.

"Hi, Willow." She gave me a welcoming head lift, moving behind the desk. "Thanks for coming. Let me just find your case notes."

While she dug through papers searching for my report, I fought the urge to flee. This woman was clearly uninterested in me, and here I was, making a fool out of myself.

I flushed, my cheeks generating enough heat to burn the building down around us.

Ren set the container on the desk, lifting the lid on one side to pull a brownie free.

"Holy shit," he barked around a mouthful, crumbs flying out of his mouth. "This is fucking amazing!"

My blush deepened. "It's the eggs. Mrs. Regis says happy hens lay joyful eggs, and those eggs make the best food."

Teddy looked up, grinning. "That makes sense. In a weird kind of way."

I felt my lips tug up into an answering grin.

"I mean if you ignore the fact the hens burned my shed down, then sure. No problem."

They both chuckled as Ren shoved the rest of the brownie in his mouth, and Teddy searched the desk for my report.

"Here we go." She pulled an envelope free from a pile of papers. "It's all in there, but just check it to make sure."

Our hands brushed as I took the envelope, a spark tingling up my arm.

Pull it together, Willow!

I ducked my head, scanning through the papers she'd handed me.

Ren shoved the container Teddy's way.

"Dude, you have to try these. They're orgasmic."

Her laugh was low and a little husky. My heart skipped a little, and I had a sudden urge to want to make her laugh.

I forced myself to continue reading the report as she lifted the lid, selecting one of the brownies.

With bated breath, I watched her lift it to her full lips, a moan escaping her as she tasted the moist, chocolatey piece of heaven.

Oh yes, I could bake a brilliant brownie.

A smirk stretched my lips. "Good?"

Teddy shook her head. "Ren's right. This is orgasmic."

An image of Teddy under me filled my head. Her hair spread out across my pillow, her lips swollen, her cheeks red and flushed as I worked her over.

I swallowed as my body reacted, clenching deliciously in response to that image.

I shuffled, clearing my throat and forcing my attention back to the report.

"This looks great, thank you," I said finally, refolding the papers and returning them to the envelope.

"If your insurance provider has any questions, the station number is on the bottom."

"Thanks."

I shifted awkwardly, glancing from Ren to Teddy, a little hesitant to be shot down in front of an audience.

"Well, thanks for this," I said again, lifting the report. "Um... I should... um... hope you enjoy the brownies. And thank you again for saving my property."

Ren laughed, snatching up the brownie container. "For these?" He gave the container a little shake. "Anytime. In fact, I might need to go have a word with your chickens about setting a few more fires if it keeps us supplied with these."

"I could... um... bring more. If you want," I said in a rush. Uncertainty had me stumbling over my words.

"Oh Gods." Teddy shoved at Ren. "Don't promise that! He'll take you up on it, and we'll never get any peace until he gets more brownies." She shot me a conspiratorial grin. "It's how he got Hannah Sharp to bake us cookies for six months. Poor woman had no idea he wasn't interested."

Ren frowned. "Who said I wasn't interested?"

Teddy gave him another shove. "Go! Go share your spoils with the boys."

He moved toward the corridor, calling over his shoulder. "Thanks, Willow! Feel free to drop these off anytime your sheds burn down."

Chuckling, I watched him leave, my amusement receding into anticipatory uncertainty when I felt Teddy's eyes on me.

I reached up, tucking hair behind my ear, the action an involuntary tell of my nervousness, the short strands barely worth the effort.

"So—"

"So—"

We both broke off, laughing.

"Sorry, you first," I said, gesturing at her to start.

"I was wondering if—"

A siren wailed in the station, interrupting her.

"Sorry, I have to go." She started moving, a mask of calm and focus falling over her face.

"Of course." I retreated. "Good luck."

I hurried outside, stepping back into the warm afternoon. Sighing, knowing I'd missed my chance, I looked back at the station, the doors to the engine bay slowly lifting.

I caught a glimpse of movement, the crew bustling about the truck, readying it for the incident call out. While I watched, Teddy appeared, pulling on a coat, her lips moving, but from this distance, I was unable to hear her. She waded into the mess of men and machines; the dance choreographed but too intricate for the untrained eye to detect.

Satisfied, they all piled into the truck, the driver setting them on their way. They pulled out, and turned away from me, heading up toward the highway.

I blew out a breath as the engine disappeared around a bend, the wail of the siren still audible.

Stay safe.

Unsure of what to do with myself, I pulled my phone from my pocket, calling my sister.

"Hello?' Honey answered.

"Hey, it's just me. I'm in town and wondered if you and Nicole want to get some lunch and hang out?" I asked, hearing my niece chattering in the background.

"Ugh, yes, but I can't. I just got called into work. One of my staff is sick, and I need to run her class. Sorry, I'd absolutely love to, but I need to find a sitter."

"Well, just call me your personal superhero, I'll take Nicole."

Honey laughed. "If you go grocery shopping for me, I'll petition the town to erect a statue in your honour."

"I'll do it. Just make sure it's bronze and captures my good side."

With my plans secured for the afternoon, I tried, unsuccessfully, to push thoughts of Captain Teresa Prince from my mind.

It's not like you really had a chance anyway.

4

Teddy

I stood in the frozen meal section of the grocery store, staring at the vast array of microwave meals knowing that no matter how exotic they sounded, they'd end up tasting like cardboard and salt.

I really need to learn to do meal prep. And learn to cook.

I thought this every time I finished a late call, bone-deep exhaustion dogging my heels.

"'Teddy?"

I twisted, blinking at the apparition before me.

"Willow?"

She pushed an overloaded cart, groceries pushed to the front while a toddler attempted to reach for them, squirming restlessly, a small carton of cereal crushed in the other.

"Hey." She sent me a smile, absently shifting a pepper away from the wiggling child. "You look...." She trailed off.

I huffed out a laugh, running a tired hand over my face. "Wrecked? Yeah. Grass fire off the highway. Likely some idiot throwing a cigarette butt out the window."

"They should be arrested. It's dry season, don't they realise how dangerous that is?"

I couldn't stop the smile that answered her outraged tone. "I appreciate that."

She shook her head, reaching for one of the doors behind which sat frozen fries and tater tots. "Please tell me you're not looking for dinner in a box."

I shrugged. "Beats cooking."

"Does it?" She tossed a packet of tater tots in the cart, nodding at the toddler when she clapped her hands excitedly.

"That's right, Nikki-Noo, these are tater tots for you," Willow sing-songed, holding up her hand for a high-five.

Nikki-Noo laughed, slapping her tiny palm against Willow's.

I grinned then turned back to consider the, no doubt, bland frozen meal options.

"Meatloaf," I decided, reaching to open the

freezer door. A hand shot out, slapping mine away.

"No way, nuh-uh." Willow shook her head vigorously. "Over my dead body, you're eating factory seconds."

"What?"

"Haven't you watched any of the food documentaries available?" She gestured at the frozen food. "So many of those boxed meats are made up of whatever bits are left over." Willow shuddered, her lips curling. "I refuse to allow you to put that crap in your mouth."

I grinned. "Yeah? So what do I do for a quick meal? A burger down at the Bronze Horseman?"

"No." She opened another door, pulling out packets of frozen peas and carrots. "I'll make you something. Tell me your address. I'll drop by in about an hour and we'll figure it out."

I blinked, then blinked again.

Is... is this happening?

"Um... sure. Do you... have your phone? I can plug my number and address in."

"Oh, good idea." She pulled a phone from her pocket, handing it over.

As I typed my information into her phone, her niece began to sing something that sounded like a mix between Humpty Dumpty and a Disney song.

"She's pretty good," I commented, handing back the phone. "Isn't her uncle a rock star?"

Willow laughed, rolling her eyes. "I mean, yes. Wolf is a rock star. But the way he is with this kid? He'd lose all street cred if anyone ever saw it."

Willow slid the phone into her back pocket, settling her hands back on the cart handle. "Alright, I'll see you in about an hour."

She nodded once, as if settling the matter, then left, heading for the register.

I watched her go, wondering if that had actually just happened or if it were a figment of my exhausted imagination.

"I should probably make dessert," I mused aloud. "You know, just in case this is real."

A woman at the far end of the aisle glanced my way, giving me raised eyebrows.

Note to self, maybe keep the musing inside. At least until after you work out if this is a date.

5

Willow

I tried not to hyperventilate as I carried the various containers up the walk to Teddy's townhouse.

You do realise you pushed your way into this date?

I swallowed the nervous giggles working their way up my throat.

If it comes down to it, you could just drop these off and run.

The door opened before I even made it halfway up her walkway.

"Hey, Willow, you came." Teddy stepped out, meeting me at the edge of her patio, taking one of the containers from my hand. "Come on in. Can I get you a drink or something?"

The Teddy of earlier that day had been transformed. Gone were her work clothes, in their place comfortable leggings, a soft shirt, and hair that had been brushed out and loosely pulled back into a ponytail.

She looks delicious.

I found my voice, mentally whipping myself over my awkwardness. "I forgot to ask if you were allergic to or don't like anything, so I made a bunch of different stuff."

"I honestly can't wait. The last meal someone cooked for me that I didn't have to pay for was with my brother after his girlfriend broke up with him." She sent me a smile. "And let's just say that he was not in the frame of mind to be doing anything but drowning his sorrows in a bottomless beer can."

Teddy led me through her house, pointing out various rooms and features as we strolled through. She had amazing taste, a kind of eclectic-meets-Scandinavian vibe. Lots of wood, cozy furnishings and textures, and the odd, unique piece – like the painting of Wonder Woman and Cat Woman kissing that hung on her kitchen wall.

"Nice painting."

She glanced at it and then burst out laughing. "Oh Gods, I'm so used to seeing it I completely forget it's there... and a little provocative." She placed the container on the kitchen counter and then began to dig through her kitchen, pulling out plates and cutlery. *Two* lots of plates and cutlery.

Guess I'm staying for dinner.

Butterflies fluttered in my stomach at her assumption.

"My brother bought it for me as a Secret Santa joke gift about a decade ago." She continued, pointing a fork at the painting in question. "I'm determined to keep it around until the perfect moment to subtly regift it to him. Preferably at his wedding – if he ever keeps a girlfriend for longer than five minutes."

"Ah, so you have one of *those* families." I opened the containers, accepting her offered serving spoons.

The word utilitarian sprang to mind when I looked around her space. Everything had a place, and there wasn't one frivolous purchase, say like an espresso machine or garlic press, to be seen.

"This smells delicious," Teddy said, surveying the options I'd prepared.

"Thanks. I like to cook." I pointed at the various containers, naming each of the dishes. "Green papaya salad, a beef noodle stir-fry. Jerk chicken – though, in full disclosure, I stole that from my sister – cornbread, peas and mashed potatoes, and some Mexican corn."

Teddy shook her head. "You need to move in, I could definitely get used to this."

We both froze, our eyes meeting across the counter. I watched as Teddy's cheeks flushed, but she held my gaze.

I cleared my throat, keeping my tone light. "Should we count this as a first date?"

Despite my tone, the question hung heavy.

"No," Teddy said slowly. "I don't think we should."

I swallowed; my appetite gone. "Okay, yeah, of course. I mean... Sorry, I just—"

"Oh no!" Teddy interrupted. "Not 'no, because I don't want to date you'. I mean 'no, because I'd like to take you on a real date'. As in, not when I'm exhausted, and you're bringing me stolen chicken."

Those bloody butterflies went into overdrive.

"Shall we say, Friday?" she asked, her gaze locked with mine.

I couldn't stop my smile. "I'd love that."

She grinned, giving a little nod. "Good. Now let's eat. I'm starving."

We served ourselves, taking a seat at her small table. Over dinner, we discussed everything from high school to favourite sports teams, politics, and beyond.

"So why Teddy?" I asked as she got a second serving of Jerk chicken.

"My brother." She rolled her eyes dramatically. "Teresa was apparently too much of a mouthful for little four-year-old Caleb, so he took to calling me Teddy. It stuck."

I tilted my head to one side, considering her. "I get it, but you're far too beautiful to be a simple Teddy."

She froze a forkful of chicken hovering in front of her mouth.

"Too much?" I asked softly.

Her lips tilted up. "Flattery may be new to me, but I'm finding I like it... coming from you."

Her voice dropped an octave, almost sounding like a purr.

"You're playing a dangerous game, Captain Prince." I raised my water glass, tilting it in her direction. "This is feeling more and more like a first date."

"Ah, my apologies. Is this where I should be an ass and kick you out before dessert?"

I chuckled, enjoying the easy banter between us. There was a dance in our interactions, a give-and-take that stripped away all pretence and left me humming with anticipation.

I want to kiss her.

I blew out a breath, pushing to my feet. "Let's get these leftovers packed up and your kitchen clean, then I need to go."

Teddy followed me into the kitchen, carrying her own plate.

"You don't want to stay and watch a movie or something?"

I turned, finding her a hair's breadth away from me.

"This is a bad idea," I whispered, pressing back against the counter. "If you're determined to wait."

"I don't know, the decision not to classify this as a first date feels pretty fucking stupid right now."

I started to laugh but froze when her hand came up to cup my cheek, her thumb brushing gently.

"Teresa..."

She moved in, her body warming mine. Her skin felt like silk as she grazed her fingers across my cheek, her gaze locked to my lips.

"Kiss me."

She leaned in, answering my whispered plea with action. Her lips brushed mine, gentle and slow, as if I were a dish she wanted to savour. I parted my lips, granting her access, and Teddy took it, her tongue dancing with mine.

We both groaned, hands coming up to fist hair, wrapping around each other.

"This. Was. A. Bad. Idea," I panted between kisses.

"Nope. Best. Idea. Ever," Teresa replied. A lock of her hair fell free to brush against my collarbone, the sensation at once too much and not enough.

"I want to taste your breasts." Fear struck as she reached for my shirt, lifting the hem a fraction before I stopped her. With a trembling hand, I pushed her back a little, creating space between us.

"Whoa," I said, desperately trying to put some distance between us. "Settle down there, Captain. At least buy a girl dinner first."

I tried to inject some humour in my voice, but it felt stiff, rough. My heart pounded; passion replaced by cold dread.

It didn't appear that Teddy noticed the shift in my mood, her eyes still glazed with passion.

"Yeah." She sucked in a breath, visibly restraining herself. "Yeah, you're right. Let me walk you out."

I had to admit, I liked how that felt, knowing she was as into me as I was into her.

Except that she doesn't know yet. She hasn't seen you.

And that thought scared the fuck out of me.

6

Willow

I'd received a text from Teddy earlier that week, officially setting the time for our first date.

TEDDY

> Look, I know this is gonna sound like a crap idea, but did you wanna come to my brother's Halloween party this Saturday? It's generally pretty fun. We do drinks, eat barbecued ribs from his smoker, there'll be a fire pit and dancing. I wouldn't normally ask, but he needs my help with set up so...

In honour of Houdini (the rooster, not the illusionist), I decided to dress as a hen. The Regis', I had discovered, had neglected to mention exactly how Houdini got his name. Or that the rooster had a strange obsession with trying to mate discarded farm tools.

Three times during the week, I'd discovered him in places he wasn't meant to be, attempting to woo all manner of equipment—the strangest being my pitchfork.

"Bye, Willow!" Dwayne, one of my employees, enthusiastically waved from the passenger seat of his mother's pick-up truck. "See you next week."

"Bye, Dwayne." I waved back, shooting his mum a smile when she gave me a wave as well.

When I'd purchased Regis Poultry Farm, I'd been told they had a work experience kid from one of the local schools. I'd assumed he was forced to be here and would drop out quickly. Then I'd met Dwayne.

Dwayne had Down Syndrome and attended the local support school where they were working with their students to transition them into employment before they left school.

Dwayne worked great with my four other employees and loved his three days on the farm. He did Thursday afternoons and Friday to Saturday. I'd already had a talk with him and his mum about offering him a full-time job when he finished school. To say he was enthusiastic about it was an understatement. He'd wrapped me in a hug, lifted me up and swung me exuberantly around.

With my plans to expand our distribution network over the next few years, I'd need good, reliable workers like Dwayne. The school had been enthusiastic about the opportunity to continue our partnership.

I glanced at my watch, making a face when I saw the time.

Crap! I'm gonna be late.

I hurriedly showered, washing the day off me, then dressed in my outfit.

Maybe I shouldn't have laughed as much as I did while sewing it last night, but I couldn't help it. This cobbled-together attempt at a 'sexy hen' was the most ridiculously amusing costume I'd ever designed.

I couldn't wait to see Teddy's reaction.

I drove myself to the address she'd given me, noting that Caleb lived in an older section of Capricorn Cove. The blocks were large, the houses small, and every yard had that settled, lived-in, established feeling.

"It's the trees," I muttered, finding a park. "I hate when there are no old trees."

I walked up to the drive, texting Teresa.

WILLOW

Hey, just arrived.

TEDDY

Great! I'll meet you at the door.

As timing would have it, I managed to arrive just as my siblings and their families did.

"Willow!" Emily pushed forward, wrapping me in a hug. "We thought you had a date tonight?"

I stepped back from my brother's wife, laughing at their couples outfits. They were dressed as a hotdog and bun.

"Nice outfit," I smirked at Calvin, enjoying his exaggerated eye-roll.

"I could say the same for you."

"Sexy chicken, right?" Honey asked, handing Tristan a fussing Nicole, who was dressed as a tiny Piglet. Tristan was a rocking Tigger, while Honey rounded out their group as Winnie the Pooh.

"Adorable," I said, leaning forward to buss Nicole on the cheek. "Best Piglet ever."

She giggled, pointing at my costume and yelling, "Chicken!"

"That's right, my little genius, Auntie Willow is a chicken."

I glanced at Emily. "No Peter tonight?" I asked, referring to my nephew.

"Collins and Nick are back in town," Calvin explained, wrapping an arm around Emily's shoulder. "They decided to do us a favour and babysit while they have a quiet night in."

Collins was Emily's sister. She was married to Nick, a billionaire who split his time between London and the Cove.

"Um, hey."

We all turned, finding Teresa standing in the open entry.

"Oh my God," I burst out, doubling over with laughter. "Perfect!"

Teresa, in a moment of unplanned brilliance provided to us by the universe, was dressed as an egg.

"Did you plan this?" Calvin asked, chuckling as he looked from Teddy to me.

"Nope." Teresa chuckled along with me. "I just thought it would be amusing."

"What came first?" Honey asked.

Teddy, I hope.

I caught Teddy's eye, finding my naughty

thoughts reflected in her gaze. A flush heat my cheeks, awareness spiking between us.

"Come on in," Teddy finally said, breaking the sudden sexual tension. "There're drinks in the kitchen and ice out back. Food is out on the back deck."

She grinned at Nicole, holding her hand up for a high-five as Tristan carried her in. "And there's a kid play area out back, complete with doting wanna-be grandmothers more than willing to watch over your precious cargo."

I loitered in the doorway, watching my family disappear into the house.

"Hey," Teddy stepped forward, wrapping an arm around my waist. "Thanks for coming."

My mind, already in the gutter, went straight back there. A delicious, throbbing ache started between my legs.

"I love Halloween, so this really isn't a hardship."

Teddy smiled, and I couldn't stop myself. I leaned forward, kissing her. For a moment, it remained chaste. A 'hello, I'm pleased to see you' kiss.

Then Teresa made a sound of pleasure, and all thoughts of decorum were lost as our mouths opened, our tongues sliding together. She backed me up, pressing me against the wall of her brother's entry, hands fisting in my short hair, her body pressing deep into mine.

More.

As if hearing my thoughts, she thrust a leg between mine, pressing her thigh up, allowing me to rock myself against it, the friction simultaneously delicious and not nearly enough.

A throat cleared behind us. As if we were teenagers caught necking by a parent, we sprang apart, cheeks flushed, lips swollen.

"I don't mean to interrupt," the guy dressed as a rat said, looking up at the ceiling, a hint of red flushing his cheeks. "But I thought I'd mention that the ribs are done and going quick."

Teddy ran a hand over her face, shooting me a grin. "Willow, this guy looking for all the world like he wants to be swallowed up is my brother, Caleb."

I held out a hand, knowing my face was as red as a beet. "Nice to meet you."

"Yeah, you too." He shook it, finally looking me in the eye. "So, ribs?"

"Sounds great."

We ate ribs with Teddy's family, I introduced her to mine. We played Halloween party games and handed out candy to the trick-or-treaters. As the party wound down, couples heading home to play out fantasies, or parents returning home to relieve babysitters, Teddy caught my hand.

"You wanna go for a stroll?"

"Sure."

Hand-in-hand, we walked past twinkling houses decorated with sheet ghosts, painted pumpkins, and fake tombstones. The night was cool but not freezing, the stars beautiful and big above us.

At the end of Caleb's street, we turned left, heading for the beach.

"I love this town," Teddy said, sucking in a deep breath. "I can't imagine living anywhere else."

I find myself liking that her roots ran deep.

"You know, I remember Honey from school but not you," she said as we reached the beach.

I kicked off my shoes, stepping into the sand.

"That's because I went to boarding school."

"Really? What was that like?"

We started walking, the sand cool under our feet.

"Wonderful. Horrible. Torture." I chuckled dryly. "Being bisexual didn't help. Kids weren't as accepting back then."

She nodded. "Yeah, I remember those days."

"My parents invested a lot of time and money in Calvin and I. Honey had been a surprise, and they just never bothered to form a bond with her." I swallowed, remembering the sickening feeling I had every time I came home. "In some ways, she got both the best and worst of it."

"What do you mean?"

I sat down, burying my feet in the sand, Teddy settling beside me, our legs brushing.

"Calvin and I had all these expectations heaped upon us. Who we would be, what we would do, who we could love." I shrugged. "Honey, they didn't care enough about to expect anything of."

"Which is its own kind of terrible."

I nodded, grateful she understood. "Yeah. For a long time, I was determined to never have kids. I worried I'd fuck them up after the upbringing I got, you know?"

Teddy nodded, her expression understanding.

"Then Honey and Tristan had Nicole, and I just... I don't know. I guess I just realised that I'm not my parents, and I could break the cycle."

"So, you're open to kids, then?"

I nodded, glancing at her. "You want them?"

"Oh yeah." She grinned. "Kids are the best. Hard work, but I love them."

We talked for a while, Teddy telling me

about her work and family, and me sharing my vision for the farm.

Hours later, as we walked hand-in-hand back to Caleb's house, I allowed myself to imagine a future with Teddy.

Halloweens like this. Christmases with babies and family. Thanksgivings and Easters, birthdays, and every ordinary day in between.

And it felt... possible.

Now I just had to get up the courage to tell her my biggest secret.

Yeah, good luck with that.

7

Teddy

I pounded on the treadmill, crushing the last five miles of my run, sweating out my frustration.

Willow's hiding something.

After no less than two months of extremely successful dates – more than one of which ended with us both falling asleep on my bed – I was still no closer to seeing her naked. Or seeing her bedroom for that matter. Which was weird, right? By date ten I'd have assumed I'd at least be invited over for coffee. But nope, here we were at the point I wouldn't consider us dating so much as together and still, not even a whisper of an invitation to her home. Instead, Willow always came to me.

Ordinarily, this kind of hang-up wouldn't bother me because, you know, consent, and boundaries, and respect for my partner, and all that. But the vibe I got off Willow wasn't "I'm not into this". Nope. Willow was right there with me.

Or she was, right up until I tried to take her clothes off. Then it all went downhill.

"Ah shit. Don't tell me she dumped you."

My heart froze at the thought.

God forbid.

As my brother took the treadmill beside mine, falling into an easy rhythm, I tried to calm my suddenly panicked heart.

Fuck. I'm falling for her.

"No," I finally retorted, sticking my tongue out at Caleb in an effort to lighten my thoughts. "Unlike you, I can keep a girlfriend."

He rolled his eyes, picking up his pace. From the corner of my eye, I saw one of the women exercising on the far side of the gym glance his way, doing a double take and beginning to openly stare.

What could I say? We were a damned attractive family.

"You'd have had a girlfriend sooner if you'd chosen to bleed blue instead of—" His lips curled as he glared pointedly at the fire truck on my chest. "That."

My brother was a cop and for some reason felt my choice to become a firefighter was a personal affront to him.

"Now, now, no need to be testy." I reached over, patting him on the shoulder. "One day you might get a promotion and become an important person in this town."

He barked out a laugh, throwing me a mock salute. "Aye, aye, Captain!"

That was my brother, silly and irreverent. And hopelessly romantic.

Maybe he could help.

I slowed my speed, moving into a sedate cooldown, considering my options.

"Just spit it out," Caleb said, pressing a button to drop his speed slightly. "You're thinking so loud they can hear it the next town over."

"It's Willow," I blurted out, unable to hold back. "She won't let me get her naked."

Caleb tripped, the treadmill continued backward while his feet went forward, upending him and sending him crashing to the floor.

"Caleb!"

"Fuck!" He pushed up as I dropped beside him, running hands over his body.

"Where does it hurt? Did you hit your head? Does your neck hurt?"

He shook his head, shifting to one side and rubbing his left ass cheek. "I hit my ass, my head is fine, and I need you to never talk about your sex life again."

"Are you okay?" The woman who'd eyed off my brother earlier crouched beside us. "I have first aid training. I can help."

He grinned, but there was none of his usual flirtation in it.

"Thanks, but the only thing damaged is my pride."

She giggled like that was the funniest thing ever.

"I'm Hannah."

"I know." He pushed to his feet. "Thanks, but I'm good."

I watched closely as he stepped back onto the treadmill, his body moving freely.

He's fine.

I glanced at Hannah and caught the surprise and hurt on her face at Caleb's gentle rejection just before she wiped her expression clean.

Long blonde hair, stunning blue-green eyes, and a body that had been made in a gym but looked like she saw some sun. I vaguely remembered her from school. She'd been a few years behind me, and a known bully. But I remembered catching her sobbing in the girls' change rooms one afternoon, looking as if her world were ending. If I'd been a better person back then I'd have asked her what was wrong. Instead, I'd stepped out, leaving her alone.

Hannah caught my glance, visibly stiffening.

"Teresa," she greeted her face now shuttered.

"Hey Hannah, good to see you."

The woman blinked, as if unused to the greeting.

"Um... yeah. You too." She pushed to her feet, dusting her knees off. "Tell Caleb he should watch for muscle strain and bruising. He hit himself pretty hard and sometimes ligament damage doesn't show up for a few days."

"Thanks, I will."

With that, she pivoted on her heel and returned to her side of the gym.

I returned to my treadmill, falling into step with Caleb.

"What was that?" I asked, tilting my head toward Hannah.

"She and Malik have a thing going on," he said, referring to one of his best friends. "I'm not getting in the middle of that."

I nodded, glancing back at the woman.

"Anyways, the fall might have done me good because I think I have a solution," Caleb declared, throwing his arms open like a showman. "Surprise date."

"Huh?"

"You show up at her place with wine, chocolates, and strawberries. You know, aphrodisiac food."

I grinned, waiting for him to continue.

"A little candlelight, a little music. You wear something... I don't know, fancy? Seductive? If it were me, I'd wear a suit or my uniform – chicks go crazy for my uniform."

I chuckled, knowing this was true considering I'd seen it happen on more than one occasion.

"And then what?"

"Then you slowly bring up the question. You work out why she keeps stopping you and then you work on breaking down that barrier."

"Gods damn it," I slapped a hand on the treadmill. "I really hate when you're entirely too wise for the body you're in."

He nodded gravely. "It is the wisdom of my ancestors... and Doctor Phil."

I laughed. "I didn't realise you were in the Daddy Phil fan club."

He shrugged. "I respect a man who can work a bald patch."

I considered Caleb's suggestion later that night as I got ready for bed.

Surprise date. I could do that.

And with plans forming, including some that stretched beyond five years, but all of which involved Willow, I fell asleep.

8

Willodean

Oh, shit.

I fumbled to a stop, staring at the gorgeous woman before me. Teresa sat on my porch swing dressed in a crisp white button-up blouse, tailored black jacket, caramel-coloured slacks, and heels. Her hair was down, the long length putting me in mind of whispered touches and frantic, hot kisses.

A cooler sat at her feet, and she looked for all the world like she belonged right there, on my porch, looking so fuckable my body ached.

That's because you love her.

"Hey," I pulled off my work gloves, hopping up the two steps to the porch. "Did we have a date tonight?"

Nervous butterflies fluttered in my stomach. Wait, did I say butterflies? I meant dragons. Massive, crazed, fire-breathing dragons.

She's totally here to break up with you.

"Nope." Teddy shoved to her feet, grinning as she closed the distance between us.

I held up my hands. "Keep back, I'm all dusty."

She laughed, leaning exaggeratedly across to kiss me. It settled like a balm on my frayed nerves.

"Good day?" she asked, resting her forehead against mine, her body still hovering away from mine.

"Getting better all the time," I answered, liking the warmth my words put in her eyes.

"Come on." She reached around, slapping me on the ass, then turned, hoisting the cooler. "I've got plans."

Teddy waited while I opened the door, shame turning my hands clammy and flushing my cheeks.

She feels like a stranger in my home.

And I guess she was. Teddy hadn't been back to my house since the great chicken fire only two months ago. It wasn't that I didn't want her here, it was just that her being in my house increased the risk of her seeing something I wasn't prepared to share.

It's not that you're not prepared to share it, it's that you're afraid of the consequences.

Yeah. That was a massive mindfuck of a hang-up.

"Come in," I said, tossing my gloves onto the entry table.

Teddy followed me into the kitchen, placing the cooler on the counter.

"Do you need me to do anything?" I asked, twisting my hands nervously.

"Relax? You're more nervous than a chicken sighting a fox."

I huffed out a laugh, forcing my shoulders to relax and rolling my eyes. "Chicken puns? Really? Our relationship must be on the rocks."

Teddy's face froze, and I immediately wished I could suck back in that last sentence, scrubbing it from existence.

"It's not," I rushed to assure her. I reached out, wrapping my arms around her and grimacing when I realised the dirt on my body was transferring to her very attractive outfit. "I'm ruining your shirt."

"I don't care, you're more important."

Teddy returned my embrace, holding me tight, her expression thoughtful.

"I know you said that we're on the rocks as a joke," she said, finally, her words delivered slowly as if she were considering each one before giving it life. "But we need to face facts. This is the first time I've come over, and I'm the one who initiated this visit. You won't let me take your clothes off, though you're more than happy to strip me naked."

I shivered, remembering two nights ago when I'd stripped her naked and then watched her wash off the grim of her day. Her hands had played over her breasts, bubbles from her body wash coating her skin, and playing peekaboo with her nipples.

"Is it me?" Teddy asked, interrupting my memory.

"What? No!" I swallowed, stepping back, hands running through my short hair. "It's...."

Come on. Just tell her.

Fear turned my blood to ice, and my body felt frozen, even as my heartbeat quickened, pounding loudly in my ears.

"Willow?"

I swallowed, my tongue thick, mouth dry. My hands shook as I reached for my shirt, pulling the ends of it free from my jeans, my fingers fumbling with the buttons.

"Willow, you don't have to—"

"I have to sh-show you," I said, my words stuttering as I sucked in rapid breaths. "Just... stay where you are. Please."

Teddy hesitated but then nodded, crossing

her arms, watching my fingers as I struggled with the buttons.

"I had a partner three years ago." I finally got the bottom button free, moving up one. "Lou. We lived together. I loved her. Thought we were going to be together forever."

My voice broke as I remembered the hurt of her leaving. "I found a rash."

I glanced up, seeing Teddy's face pale, her lips pressed together in a thin line. "Breast cancer. She was the first person I told. And for a long while the only one because she bailed on me the day after I found out. Less than twenty-four hours after confiding in her." My hands halted at the button at my sternum. "I've never heard from Lou again."

"Willow..." Teddy shifted, reaching for me.

I held up a hand, halting her movement. "Just... stay there a moment. Otherwise, I won't get this out."

I undid the last three buttons, holding my shirt closed.

"Chemotherapy took my hair. I'm technically no longer a blonde, but lucky for me, we have bleach, and I rock a pixie cut."

A ghost of a smile touched her lips, answering my attempt at humour.

"I've been cancer-free for twelve months. Maybe it was crazy to buy a chicken farm. But I needed to come back. I needed to get out of New York and come home. I wanted to be here to see my nieces and nephews grow up. I wanted roots."

I sucked in a breath, admitting something I'd never dared to say, even to myself. "And I wanted a legacy. I wanted something that would continue after I was gone. I wanted to put my mark on history."

"And a chicken farm does that for you?" Teddy asked, no judgment on her face.

I laughed, shaking my head. "No, actually, I have no idea what will do that. But it seemed like a good idea at the time."

She chuckled, shifting slightly toward me.

It's now or never, Willodean.

I peeled back the sides of my shirt, pulling it free and dropping it on the kitchen floor. "I had to have a double mastectomy. The cancer was only in one breast, but the risk was high, so they recommended I remove both breasts."

I reached for the clasp at the front of my bra, unhitching it. "This is what I look like now."

The bra with its fake boob fillets fell away, revealing a scar-marked chest. I no longer had nipples or breast tissue, just painful pink scars that were slowly fading on my flat chest.

I held my hands out to the side, showing Teddy my body. "They offered me a breast reconstruction, but I didn't want it. Surgery after surgery? No thanks." I swallowed, fighting to find the words. "I know it's not what you wanted, but—"

"What I wanted?" Teddy asked, her voice hoarse. "What exactly do you think I want, Willow?"

I fought the desire to cover my scars, clenching my fists to keep my hands in place. "I don't know, someone who is double-breasted? Someone who isn't damaged goods?"

She didn't answer, just stepped forward, cupping the back of my head and bringing my lips to hers.

It was a demanding kiss. Hungry and full of heat.

"You're perfect," Teddy told me as she shrugged off her jacket. "Fucking perfect."

My fingers delved into her hair, my body pressing against hers as she fumbled with my pants, unbuttoning the jeans and shoving them down.

"Where?" she asked between kisses.

"Lounge," I told her, knowing I wouldn't be able to make it to the bedroom.

In a fumbling stumble, we shed our clothes, both of us naked.

She pushed me down on the lounge,

spreading my thighs, her body sliding down mine until she kneeled between my thighs.

"You're beautiful, Willow." She lifted up, peppering kisses down my neck and across my collarbone before hovering above a pinched scar. "Fucking perfect."

Her lips pressed over the damaged tissue, kissing from one end of the scar to the other.

My heart pounded in my ears, a tiny part of me wondering if this was nothing more than a pity fuck before she dumped me tomorrow.

God, I hated the fear and uncertainty that churned in my gut, distracting me from being in this moment.

"Okay," Teddy rocked back on her heels, and I took a moment to admire the planes and curves of her body.

My woman is fit.

"Okay?" I asked, forcefully tearing my gaze from her powerful biceps and glorious breasts to look into her eyes.

"That's the expression I like to see," she said with a grin, touching a finger to my nose. "Not the 'I wanna be into this but am pretty sure you're gonna walk out on me' one you were wearing."

I huffed, shaking my head. "How did you know?"

"You have zero poker face. Promise to never

play with my brother, he'll clean you out, and I just don't think he'd make a good farmer."

I barked out a laugh.

Teresa cupped my chin, holding my gaze, her expression warm but serious.

"This." She ran the thumb of her free hand over a scar. "Doesn't make you anything but a survivor, Willow. You're strong, you're powerful, you beat fucking cancer."

I grinned, tears dotting my lashes.

"I'm proud of you. And so fucking thankful that I'm able to be here with you right now."

She leaned in, the kiss warm and gentle.

Words that felt too soon to say, burned on the tip of my tongue.

I love you.

I swallowed them, using the kiss to communicate what I couldn't yet say.

Teddy drew back, brushing a stray tear from my cheek. "I love you, Willodean. I know that seems soon, but—"

I shook my head, laughter spilling from my lips as I shifted, my hand lifting her breasts, pressing urgent kisses to them.

"I love you too," I told her between kisses. "It's not too soon. It feels..."

"Perfect," she answered, finishing my sentence.

Her head tipped back, her chest pushing

out toward me, and that was the end of our declarations for now.

I sucked her right breast into my mouth, palming her left breast.

"Oh God," Teddy groaned, her hands digging into my hair. "This was meant to be about you."

I chuckled, flicking her nipple with my tongue, loving how sensitive Teddy was to my touch.

"Do you want me to stop?" I asked, moving across to her left breast, gently grazing my thumb over her right nipple.

She made a sound like a protest and a plea, my body clenching in response, hot wet, slicking my thighs.

"Stand up," I ordered, reaching down to frame my hands around her hips. "I want to taste you."

Teddy rose up, her hands settling on my shoulders. Gently, I moved her legs, opening her to my gaze. I ran my fingers through her wet curls, groaning as her scent intensified.

"Oh," I whispered, grazing my fingers up and down her lips, gently cupping her. "You're beautiful, Teresa."

Using both hands to part her, we both moaned as my fingers danced through her slick heat.

Unable to deny us any longer, I leaned forward, my tongue finding her clit, getting my first taste of Teddy. Nothing could have prepared me for her taste, her scent, or the beauty of her reaction.

I eagerly tasted her, desperate for more. Desperate to hear her sweet little pants and whispered filthy demands.

"More," she ordered, her hips shifting under my tongue, her body beginning to ride my mouth. "There, there, there, there!" she chanted, her body shaking as I drove her higher.

I curled a finger into her, gently sucking on her clit.

Her pussy milked my finger, her body bucking as she reached her peak, riding my face, desperately fucking my finger.

"Yes!" She came, legs trembling, her fingernails digging into my shoulders.

I eased her onto the couch, laughing when she reached for me, greedily kissing me.

"Mm, you taste good."

I chuckled, palming her ass. "That would be you, Captain Prince."

She snuggled in, her hands drifting down my body. "Do I get to return the favour now?"

"Um, if you'd like."

Teddy laughed, pressing me down onto the

couch, settling over me. She began much the way I had, with kisses and gentle touches.

I sighed, closing my eyes as she worked her way down my body.

Her fingers parted me, and she hovered for a moment, her breath hot on my centre.

"Gonna see how many times I can make you come," Teddy said, shooting me an evil grin just before her mouth closed over me, hot, wet and talented.

My hands fisted in the couch cushions, my body twisting and turning as Teddy's relentless mouth touched me in all the ways I'd imagined.

My body throbbed, burning with desire, deep, long moans escaping from between my lips. Teresa brought her fingers up, dancing them along my labia before dipping between to roll over my clit.

"Oh God," I breathed, arching into her. "Yes, babe. Do that again."

She answered my demand with a heavenly roll of her fingers, my body clenching in response.

As if she knew exactly what I liked, Teresa set a rhythm designed to break me, teasing and licking, her tongue and fingers working in tandem, I lost my battle with control, my body shaking, curses and praise falling from my lips as I finally, finally suffered that sweet bliss.

Teddy rested her head on my abdomen, licking her lips. "Delicious."

I shuddered, loving her rapt expression. "That was..."

She chuckled. "I know."

We lay there for a minute, just catching our breath and looking at each other.

"Again?" she asked, her hand dropping to stroke my belly.

"Can I have a shower first? I'm still dusty." I lifted a hand to brush my hair back from my face. "And now sweaty and sticky."

"Only if I can join you." She sat up, holding out a hand to pull me to a seat beside her. "Let me put the food from the cooler in the fridge first."

"I'll do it," I kissed her shoulder, getting up from the couch. "My 'room is down the hall to the left if you want to start the shower in the master."

Teresa wiggled her eyebrows. "Choosing the bathroom closest to a bed, are we?"

I kissed her, tasting the laughter on her lips. "Of course. You didn't fall in love with a stupid woman."

Her face softened, her hand caressing my hip. "No, I certainly didn't."

We separated, Teresa heading for the bathroom, me for the kitchen. I began to put away the cooler food items, smiling at the clothes scattered across the floor.

Who would have thought I'd enjoy being a nudist?

"Um, Willow?" Teresa called from the bedroom.

"Yeah?" I called back, pausing with a tub of strawberries in my hand as I waited for her reply.

"I don't mean to pry, but...." She poked her head out the bedroom door, her long brunette strands dancing with her movement. "Why is there a giant cock in your bedroom?"

For a moment, I blinked, confused. Then realisation struck, and I bowed over, doing that strange thing where someone is so struck with hilarity that they end up sounding a little like an asthmatic seal.

"Oh, Gods!" I lifted a hand, wiping tears from my eyes. "I'm so sorry. I didn't even think."

I popped the strawberries in the fridge and then headed down the hall, still chuckling. Teresa shifted, backing into the room, her arms crossed, amusement on her face.

In the corner of my bedroom stood the six-foot-high metal statue my sister-in-law, Emily, had made.

"Teresa, meet Cocky." I giggled, nearly losing my composure once again. "He's a house-warming gift from my family. You have Wonder Woman; I have a giant cock."

Teddy lifted one arm, making an exaggerated show of wiping her brow. "Phew! You know, I'm pretty open sexually, but if that had been some kind of kink fetish, I might have needed to reconsider my assumptions about you."

I burst out laughing, experiencing a freedom in that moment I hadn't felt before.

"Is this why you never invited me over?" she asked, eyebrows raised in question.

"Ah, no. It was the fear you might see the old photos of me around the house or find one of my boob fillet bras and work out that I'm damaged goods."

Teddy closed the gap between us, roughly pulling me into her.

"You're not damaged," she told me, voice fierce. "You're fucking perfect. I love you."

"I love you too," I whispered, our mouths finding each other, our tongues dancing.

Here I stood, in my bedroom naked and unashamed, with a giant rooster statue watching us, a gorgeous woman in my arms, and no tits.

I could honestly say I'd never been happier.

EPILOGUE 1

Teddy

I shuffled nervously from one foot to the other, pulling at the collar of my dress.

"Calm down," Caleb told me from his reclined position on the porch swing. "It's all gonna be okay."

"Easy for you to say," I retorted, scowling in his direction. "You're already married."

"Yeah, I am," he agreed easily. "Best decision ever."

I didn't bother to answer, nerves twisting in my belly.

A car turned into the drive, bouncing up the gravel toward the house.

"Shit, she's here."

"Breathe, Teresa." My brother's hand settled on my shoulder. "You got this."

Honey sent me a bright grin from the driver's seat, a blindfolded Willow in the passenger seat. I saw her lips move and Honey laugh as she put the car in park.

I stepped down, immediately making a beeline for her door. I opened it, reaching out to take her hand.

"Hey, babe. I got you. Just follow me."

Willow's face was flushed, her cheeks pink, her lips in a small grin. "What are you up to, Teresa Prince?"

"You'll see."

In the distance, one of the roosters crowed.

"Do I get a clue?" she asked as I helped her from the car.

"Hmm." I pretended to think for a moment. "How about it involves Cocky."

I guided her up the stairs of our home, holding the door open for her.

"Should I suspect *fowl* play?" she asked, a teasing note in her tone.

I barked out a laugh, loving this woman with all my heart.

"Perhaps," I hedged, leading her down the hall into our bedroom. Inside, I moved her just so, nodding at my brother who'd taken up position across the room.

He shot me a grin, holding the camera at the ready. Behind us, Honey did the same, her smile big, her eyes a little wet, her hands steady as she began to record.

"Okay, you can take the blindfold off now."

Willow lifted it, glancing around, spotting me first, her smile big and beautiful.

"What are we—" she choked, her eyes widening as she spotted the second giant rooster statue in the room, a sign hung from his neck, the letters printed in thick, black cursive.

Will you marry me?

"What did you do!?" she squealed, laughter spilling out.

I dropped to one knee, nerves making my palms sweat. Willow's eyes widened, her beautiful eyes meeting mine, shock, surprise, and pleasure reflected in their magnificent depths.

"Willodean Jameson," I began, my voice hoarse with emotion. "Will you do me the honour of—"

"Yes!" she squealed, dropping to her knees and throwing her arms around me. "Yes! Yes! Yes!"

"I didn't even get to ask!" I protested, dropping the ring box and falling backward onto the floor as she pressed kisses all over my face.

Willow drew back slightly, cupping my face, her expression radiant. "I love you, Teresa. You are the best thing that has ever happened to me. I can't wait for you to be my wife."

With a laugh, I kissed her, our joy spilling over.

And much to my brother's dismay, Willow insisted we call the second rooster statue Ring.

EPILOGUE 2

Willow

I pulled Teddy's leg onto my lap, my thumbs gently rubbing her swollen ankles.

"God that's good," she moaned, her head falling back. "I can't believe how swollen I am. I finally understand what women mean when they say pregnancy made them feel like a whale."

I chuckled, pressing a kiss to her big toe. "If it helps, you're a beautiful whale."

She tossed a throw pillow at my head, sticking her tongue out at me. "It doesn't."

Teddy was overdue by three days with our first.

"How are the contractions?"

"Still thirty apart," she admitted, grimacing. "It'd be nice if our little girl decided to hurry up."

I reached out, rubbing her stomach. "Okay little Henny-Penny, you heard Momma. It's time to come out and meet us."

"If that worked, she'd have been here last—"

Liquid soaked through her dress.

"Are you kidding me?" Teddy demanded, struggling to push up to sitting. "Oh my Gods."

"It's just your water breaking, baby." I reached down, helping her to sit, gently rubbing her back. "Let me get your bag ready, notify the doctor and we'll keep monitoring. What's our agreement?"

"Twenty minutes apart," Teddy said, reaching for her phone.

"Good."

Hours later, an exhausted, sweaty, magnificent Teresa pushed our little girl into the world. She had a shock of black hair, a tiny button nose, and a set of lungs that would make Houdini proud.

"Oh, she's beautiful," I sobbed, accepting her from the doctor. I placed her on Teddy's chest, both of us sobbing as she settled, her cries quieting.

"Welcome to the world, Lizzy."

I kissed Teddy's forehead, brushing sweaty

strands from her face. "Thank you, baby. Thank you for our beautiful daughter and wonderful life."

"I love you," she said, tears streaking down her face.

"I love you too. Thank God for Satanic fire-starting chickens."

Laughing, we cuddled, falling in love with our beautiful daughter.

***

I hope you loved Teddy and Willow!
They were absolutely egg-cellent to write!
Be sure to check out their bonus slice of life on my website.

Next up is Caleb and his lady love!
You can continue the entire series by checking them out on my website at
www.EvieMitchell.com

If you enter the code EBOOK10 you can get 10% off your purchase from my website.

ABOUT THE AUTHOR

Evie Mitchell is a thirty-something romance author (she/her/hers) living with disability. She believes in inclusion, accessibility, and fierce romance. Her loves include steamy romance novels, her husband, their THREE sausage dogs (heaven help her), and her ever-growing collection of book-related mugs.

As a woman with a diverse work history including in areas such as emergency response, event management, human rights, disability access, and security - her books are filled with true stories (bridezillas), worst-case scenarios (malfunctioning dresses), and her favourite tropes (one-bed).

Evie specialises in fiercely inclusive happily ever afters.

ALSO BY EVIE MITCHELL

Capricorn Cove Series

The Shake-Up

Double the D

Muffin Top

The Mrs. Clause

New Year Knew You

Double Breasted

As You Wish

You Sleigh Me

Resolution Revolution

Meat Load

Larsson Siblings Series

Thunder Thighs

Clean Sweep

The X-list

Reality Check

The Christmas Contract

Dogg Pack Books

Puppy Love

Bad English

The Frock Up

Pier Pressure

All Access Series

Knot My Type

Love Flushed

Nameless Souls MC Series

Runner

Wrath

Ghost

Shield

Elliot Security Series

Rough Edge

Bleeding Edge